Disney's

DOUG™

Created by
Jim Jinkins

CHRONICLES

Doug
Rules

by Nancy Krulik

Illustrated by Brian Donnelly and Tony Curanaj

Doug Rules is hand-illustrated by the same
Grade A Quality Jumbo artists who bring you
Disney's Doug, the television series.

Disney
PRESS

New York

Original characters for "The Funnies" developed by Jim Jinkins and
Joe Aaron.

Printed in the United States of America.

3 5 7 9 10 8 6 4

The artwork for this book is prepared using watercolor.

The text for this book is set in 18-point New Century Schoolbook.

Library of Congress Catalog Card Number: 98-87731

ISBN: 0-7868-4297-0

For more Disney Press fun visit www.DisneyBooks.com.

Created by
Jim Jinkins

CHRONICLES

Doug
Rules

CHAPTER ONE

Slam!

Doug Funnie let the door swing shut as he ran out onto the sidewalk. "Sorry I'm late," Doug apologized to his best pal, Skeeter Valentine. "I overslept."

"That's okay, man," Skeeter

replied. "As long as we get to school by the bell, we won't be late. That's the rule."

Doug walked faster. He had gym first period. Doug definitely didn't want to miss one minute of gym. They were having a sit-up competition. Doug was good at sit-ups. He was practically a sit-up machine! Today just might be the day he broke the school record.

The bell rang just as Skeeter and Doug reached the locker room. Coach Spitz blew his whistle—loudly—right in Doug's ear. "Five minutes!" he shouted.

Skeeter reached into his gym

bag and pulled out his uniform—
sneakers, gray shorts, and a
white T-shirt. Doug reached into
his bag and pulled out . . . a black

3

leotard, black tights, a black beret, and a pair of black ballet slippers. *Oh, no!* Doug had been in such a rush, he'd grabbed his older sister Judy's backpack by mistake. This was her costume for her school play. Doug wasn't sure what Judy was going to be in the play, but whatever it was, it was depressing.

Doug threw the costume back in the bag. No way was he doing his sit-ups in those things! Imagine what Roger Klotz would say if he saw Doug with ballet stuff!

Suddenly, the boys heard a loud thud. They raced to see what had happened. Doug looked into the

supply room and spotted Coach
Spitz lying on the floor, all tan-
gled up in volleyball nets. He

looked like a bug trapped in a giant spiderweb.

All the boys were quiet. Then someone let out a huge guffaw. Doug recognized the laugh. It belonged to Roger Klotz.

"You think this is a joke, Klotz?" the coach asked.

"That was Funnie," Roger said, pointing to Doug.

"What's so funny about this?" Coach Spitz said.

"Not funny, Coach. I mean Funnie . . . Doug Funnie," Roger explained.

"It wasn't me," Doug insisted. "You're the one who laughed, Roger."

But the coach didn't care who laughed. He'd just noticed Doug. "Where are your gym clothes, Funnie?" Coach Spitz asked. "Without gym clothes, you don't play. That's the rule."

"But Coach, it's sit-up day," Doug pleaded. "It's not like the seat of my pants will scratch up the gym floor."

Coach Spitz shook his head. "A rule is a rule."

"Rules!" Doug muttered as he watched his friends run onto the gym floor.

After gym class, Doug went to his

locker to get his banjo. It was time for band practice.

"Hey, Doug dude, off to practice?" Skunky Beaumont called out. Skunky was holding his drumsticks in his right hand.

"Where are your drums, Skunky?" Doug asked him.

Skunky looked up. He looked down. He looked behind himself. "Oops. I knew I forgot something," Skunky replied. "Be right back."

Doug was about to tell Skunky to hurry. Mr. Fort had a rule about getting to band practice on time. But Doug knew Skunky wouldn't care.

Doug reached the field just in

time. Mr. Fort began conducting the school fight song. As Doug played his part, he tapped his left foot to the beat.

"Mr. FUNNIE!" Suddenly Mr. Fort stopped conducting and called out Doug's name from the podium.

"Uh, yes, Mr. Fort?" Doug asked sheepishly.

"You know you are supposed to tap with your right foot—always! That is the rule."

Doug gulped. "But Mr. Fort, I'm left-handed . . . and footed!"

"Funnie!" Mr. Fort ordered. "Drop and give me twenty!"

Doug was shocked. What kind of goof-o rule was that? What did it matter if you tapped your left foot—as long as you kept the beat?

But there was no arguing. Doug got on his hands and knees and started doing push-ups.

"I hate rules!" Doug groaned as he moved his body up and down.

For the rest of the morning, Doug stewed about how a couple of dopey rules had ruined his day. "Why couldn't I do those sit-ups in my street clothes?" he complained to Skeeter at lunch. "It wouldn't have hurt his crummy old floor!"

Patti and Beebe joined them at their table. "Doug, they'll have another sit-up contest in a month or two. You can beat the record then," Patti said, trying to cheer him up.

"Well, for once, I agree with him," said Beebe. "I wish the rule about having to take tests was gone so I wouldn't have to learn all those math formulas! In fact, I wish *all* rules were canceled, as of now!"

Doug felt worse than ever. He'd forgotten about the math test tomorrow. Now he had something else to worry about!

The afternoon was no better. As Doug trudged home, dreading all the studying he had to do, he couldn't stop thinking about what Beebe had said. What if there were no rules? He imagined a home without rules. He could play ball in the house, and he would never have to help his father mow the lawn.

And if there were no rules in the whole *universe,* the earth wouldn't have to turn on its axis. It could be summer all year round! There would be no laws of gravity; everyone could fly wherever they wanted to! Doug pictured himself floating up into the sky, and playing the banjo with some musical Martians!

"Hey Dougie, dreaming of little what's-her-name?"

Judy's taunting voice woke

Doug from his daydream. He real-
ized he had slowed to a complete
stop right in front of their yard.
They walked into the house
together.

"You look like you've got a lot on your mind, little brother," Judy said. "What's up?"

"Aw, it's nothing," Doug answered. "I just have a math test . . . and I have to make at least a B on it to stay in band. It's a school rule."

"Well, you'd better quit gathering rosebuds. The sands of time are running apace, and math is not your best subject," Judy warned. "And here's another rule for you: No study . . . no passee!"

Doug sighed. A world without rules was seeming better and better every minute.

CHAPTER TWO

X equals the square root of . . .
Doug yawned as he read the first
math problem on the page. Math
always made him tired. The num-
bers were dancing in front of his
eyes—21 doing the tango with 42,

and 63 doing the funky chicken with 89. Before long Doug was fast asleep at his desk.

Doug dreamed that he was walking up to the school. Just as his left foot stepped through the doorway, music blared from the loudspeaker. Balloons and colorful confetti fell from the ceiling. Principal White leaped out from behind the trophy case and handed Doug a key to the faculty restroom.

"Congratulations, Young Person," the principal said in a booming voice. "You are the one millionth person to enter our beloved school. In honor of this

occasion, you will become
Principal for a Day, starting now!"

Doug was shocked. "Principal
for a Day? I must be dreaming!"
Doug exclaimed.

"Yes, you are," Principal White
agreed.

"What does being Principal for a
Day mean?" asked Doug.

"As principal, you're the Big
Cheese. Master of the Universe.
The Rulemeister."

Doug smiled as it dawned on
him. "You mean I get to make the
rules?" he asked.

"Precisely," said Principal
White.

"Then I have just one rule for

this school," Doug announced. "As long as I am principal, there will be . . . NO RULES!"

Everyone cheered. Some of the kids put Doug on their shoulders and carried him around the cafeteria.

"Remember the fun you're having now," Principal White shouted to the students. "And tell your parents to vote for me."

But no one heard the principal. They were too busy cheering. Doug grinned and waved to his fans. A school with no rules! This was going to be the best day of his life. Doug was sure of it.

CHAPTER THREE

Later that morning, as Principal Funnie roamed the halls of his school, Skunky came zooming by on his in-line skates. " 'Scuze me, Doug dude," Skunky said. "I'm in a hurry. I'm really late."

Doug smiled. "Relax, Skunky. You *can't* be late. There's no rule saying you have to be on time."

Skunky came to a quick stop. But much to Doug's surprise, he did not seem happy. "No rules? Whoa man, there *have* to be rules! How else will I know what *not* to do? Dude! I *need* those rules!"

As Skunky rolled off, Doug could hear the shouts of kids playing basketball in the gym. He grinned. He was about to shoot hoops in his street clothes. There was nothing the coach could do about it!

"Heads up!" Chalky yelled as a

ball flew past Doug's head. Three
players dived for the ball. One
guy grabbed it. The others
pounced on him and started
wrestling for control.

"Hey, Coach, that's a foul, isn't it?" Chalky shouted to Coach Spitz.

The coach shook his head helplessly and stared down at his gym floor.

"Look at those scratches. They've wiped the finish right off the wood with their shoes and boots," Coach Spitz told Doug. He wiped a tear from his eye. "I can't stand by and watch this happen. I gotta get outta here." The coach sadly walked out of the gym.

Just then Doug heard screams coming from the cafeteria. He raced in to see what was happening.

"Food fight!" somebody yelled.
Splat! A chocolate cream pie
slammed Doug in the face.

"Hey! Who did that?" Doug asked as he wiped the cream from his eyes. "It's not . . . whoa!!!!!" Before he could finish his sentence, Doug's shoe hit a banana peel. Principal Funnie slid head-first across the cafeteria!

Doug came to a stop at a table at the far end of the room where Roger was sitting behind a heaping tray of chocolate peanut butter brownies.

"Hey, Funnie, I gotta admit, this no rules thing was the smartest idea you've ever had. Of course, it's the only *good* idea you've ever had," Roger complimented Doug.

"Uh, gee, thanks. . . I think,"

Doug replied. "Hey, Roger, you're
not going to eat *all* those brownies, are you?"

"Yes I am. You said there were
no rules," Roger sneered. "No
rules means no sharing in my

book. Unless you're going to make a rule about it."

Doug shook his head. "I just thought you might not want to eat so many," he said.

Just then Beebe passed by. Her hair was covered with whipped cream, and she was headed toward Principal White at the table next to Roger. "You've got to do something," Beebe told the ex-mayor. "How could you let these little monsters ruin my expensive hairdo?!"

"Sorry. My hands are tied," Principal White said. He pointed to Doug. "As long as this Young Person is in charge, we have to . . .

uh . . . it's important that we . . . now, what was your question again?"

Before Beebe could answer, a Tarzan-like yell came from above. Skunky flew overhead, swinging from a rope he'd attached to the beams of the cafeteria.

"It's bungee time!" he shouted. "Hey, Doug, I'm in real trouble for this one, right?"

Doug shook his head. "No way, Skunky," Doug called up to him. "You can't get in trouble in a school with no rules."

Skunky sadly swung down to the ground, untied the rope, and walked away.

This "no rules" thing was not turning out the way Doug had planned. Still, no rules were better than rules. Doug was sure of it.

Sort of.

CHAPTER FOUR

Doug really needed some peace and quiet so he could think things through. He found it in Ms. Kristal's English classroom. *All* of the classrooms were quiet— no students had been in them all day. And since there were no rules, they didn't have to go to detention hall for skipping, either!

Doug sat at a desk in the back of the room and rested his head in his hands. It felt good to be alone for a few minutes.

But Doug *wasn't* alone. There, in the front of the room, Doug saw something he never thought he'd see in a million years. Skunky was sitting at a desk, quietly reading a book!

"Principal Funnie, dude, this no rules thing is not cool," Skunky said, turning around in his chair. "Now *everyone* is just hanging out. I can't find a rule to break, so I'm reading. Whoa, man, it's soo-o-o confusing!"

Wow! Skunky reading! He must have been really desperate.

"I'm sorry, Skunk," Doug apologized.

Just then, Ms. Kristal jogged quickly into the room. She leaped up, did a back flip off one of the desks, and announced, "I have an exciting lesson planned today, students! It's spelling rules day! Wowee!"

Ms. Kristal pulled out a jump rope. "*I* before *E* except after *C*," she chanted to the beat as she jumped. "Unless sounded

as *A* like in *neighbor* and
weigh."

"Uh, excuse me, Ms. Kristal,"
Doug interrupted her. "But there
are no rules today."

Ms. Kristal stopped jumping. "Not even in spelling?" she asked.

Doug shook his head.

"But that means everyone will spell words differently," Ms. Kristal said. "How can anyone read what others have written?"

Doug had no answer. She definitely had him there. But a promise *was* a promise. And he had said no rules for as long as he was principal.

Doug looked over to see if Skunky had caught Ms. Kristal's jump rope act. But Skunky was too busy reading his book to notice anything else.

Things were getting seriously weird.

Doug's head was pounding. He needed some fresh air—bad. He rushed out of the classroom and walked outside to the sports field. *Whoosh!* A huge beetball whizzed by and bonked him on the head.

"Oops, sorry, Doug," Patti said, as she walked over to him. "Hey, I've been looking for you. How about we make one rule? We play beetball—only beetball—by the rules."

Doug shook his head. "Patti, I wish I could, but . . ."

"*Doug*. Without rules, balls are strikes and outs are safe," Patti

37

urged. "Without rules, nobody wins!"

Doug knew Patti made sense. But he also knew he couldn't start making rules now.

"Patti, how can I change now, after I promised there'd be no rules?" Doug asked.

"Well, if there are no rules, then I'm at bat all the time," Patti declared. She picked up her bat and began whacking beetballs across the field. She hit them high. She hit them low. Doug had to duck behind the backstop to keep from being beaned. The beetballs whizzed by at lightning speed. There were beetballs flying

everywhere. There were beetballs
in the trees, and beetballs on the
school walks.

* * *

Doug's world had turned upside down. Roger actually thought Doug had a great idea. Skunky was reading books. And now, even his beloved Patti Mayonnaise was furious at him!

At least Doug knew *Skeeter* was happy. He'd spent the whole day in the science lab—by himself. For once he didn't have to get a teacher to supervise him, because there were no rules. Doug rushed inside to find Skeeter. He really needed to see a friendly face.

As Doug ran down the hall, he bumped into Roger. But Doug

almost didn't recognize him. Roger was huge! His black leather jacket was covered in brown chocolate frosting. His hair was blanketed in thick, gooey chocolate. And there was a big pile of peanuts on his nose. *Roger was turning into a giant human brownie!*

"This is all your fault, Funnie," the Roger-brownie moaned. "If you hadn't come up with the loony idea for a school without rules, I wouldn't have eaten all those brownies. Now look at me. I'll get you for this!"

Well, Doug thought, as he ran down the hallway, at least one

thing was back to normal: Roger
was mad at him.

As Doug reached the door of the

science lab, he called to Skeeter. "Hey, buddy, how's it going?" he asked.

"GET OUT OF THE WAY, DOUG!!!!!" Skeeter shouted. "My experiment! It's going to blow!!!!!!"

KABOOM! Doug and Skeeter dived for cover, just as Skeeter's latest science experiment exploded.

CHAPTER FIVE

"Eeeew! Skeeter, what is that?"
Doug asked as he held his nose
and stumbled into the hall.

"Vinegar, hydrochloric acid, and
a flower," Skeeter replied, holding
his shirt over his face. "I was

trying to invent a new perfume for Beebe's birthday."

"Well, you stunk up the school," the giant Roger-brownie shouted as he rolled toward the exit.

Doug heard footsteps coming down the hall. "STAMPEDE!" Chalky yelled as he led a pack of kids toward the doors. "Let's get out of here!"

"What are you going to do, Doug?" Skeeter asked.

"I have an idea," Doug answered. "RUN!!!" The two boys raced down the hall, passing the other nose-holding kids storming out of the school.

By the time Doug and Skeeter

reached the school's front lawn,
the Skeeter stench had become
big news! Ambulances and fire
trucks were screeching down the
street toward the school. News
vans were parked along the
sidewalk.

"Are you the man in charge here?" a TV reporter asked Principal White.

Principal White looked into the camera, wiped the sweat from his brow, and gulped. "Uh, no, sir, not today, not me," he stammered. The principal looked through the crowd and spotted Doug. He pointed right at Doug. "He is! There's the man in charge. Talk to him. Principal Dave Funnie."

The news reporter turned to Doug. In an instant, Doug was completely engulfed by camera-men, and reporters with micro-phones. Sweat began to pour off him. Lights flashed in his face.

The reporters shouted their questions so fast he couldn't quite understand. "Why aren't the kids in class? Where are the teachers?

What happened? *WHO'S RESPONSIBLE??!!!"*

Suddenly, everything stopped at once. The entire crowd of people began to point at the one who *was* responsible and to chant his name: "Doug! Doug! Doug! Doug . . ."

CHAPTER SIX

"Doug! Doug! Wake up!"
Doug sat up and rubbed the sleep
from his eyes. Judy stood over
him, shaking his shoulders.
"I must have fallen asleep. I was

having this dream. . . ." Doug told
her.

"It sounded like a doozy," Judy
said.

"It didn't start out that way,"
Doug explained. "But things got
out of hand."

"Ooooh, sounds interesting," Judy replied. "Tell me about it."

Doug shook his head. "Not right now, Judy. I need to study for that test tomorrow so I can stay in the band. There are rules about these things, you know."

The next morning Doug aced his math test. He was so happy that during band practice, he was daydreaming about Patti swooning and saying, "Oh, Doug! You're so . . . mathematical-y!" Suddenly, he heard Mr. Fort's voice booming out his name.

"Not FUNNIE!" the band director shouted. "You missed

your cue! You know the rule. Drop and give me twenty!"

Doug wasn't happy about having to do twenty push-ups in front of everyone. But he knew there was a reason for Mr. Fort's rule about everyone playing his instrument at the right time. Otherwise the band would sound like a noisy, banging racket. Everything would be a big mess.

Sort of like a school without rules.